Apple Picking Time

by Michele Benoit Slawson   illustrated by Deborah Kogan Ray

Dragonfly Books™   Crown Publishers, Inc. • New York

For Horatio
M. B. S.

For Raymond
D. K. R.

DRAGONFLY BOOKS™ PUBLISHED BY CROWN PUBLISHERS, INC.

Published by Crown Publishers, Inc., a Random House company, 201 East 50th Street, New York, NY 10022

CROWN is a trademark of Crown Publishers, Inc.

www.randomhouse.com/kids/

Library of Congress Cataloging-in-Publication Data
Slawson, Michele Benoit.
Apple picking time / by Michele Benoit Slawson ; illustrated by Deborah Kogan Ray.
p.   cm.
Summary: A young girl and her family spend a fall day picking apples with others from their small town.
[1. Apple—Harvesting—Fiction.] I. Ray, Deborah Kogan, 1940– ill. II. Title.
PZ7.S63124Ap   1994
[E]—dc20   92-23400

ISBN 0-517-58971-0 (trade)
0-517-88575-1 (pbk.)

First Dragonfly Books™ edition: August 1998

10 9

DRAGONFLY BOOKS is a trademark of Alfred A. Knopf, Inc.

Sometime after the summer is spent but before the jack-o'-lanterns are lit,

it's apple picking time. All over the valley, up and down the hillsides,

the branches are heavy with red apples. Tomorrow we will go to work.

When it's apple picking time, everyone has to help. The whole town knows we have only three weeks to get the fruit off the trees before it spoils. Papa takes time off from the market, Mama leaves the housework, and I don't have to go to school. Even the Sisters from the convent help at harvest time.

When you go apple picking, you have to get up before the sun. The moon is still high in the sky, and the rooster hasn't crowed yet. The birds are asleep. Everything is asleep—except Mama, Papa, and me, and all the other apple pickers.

We meet outside the town in cars and pickups. Papa finds a place behind Grandma and Grandpa's truck. Then our families follow the narrow dirt road to the orchards. We travel past fallen cornstalks, fields of hay, and mailboxes with their flags up. If we hit a bump, the lights bounce from the road and we are in darkness again.

Mama and Papa talk in low voices and I draw faces on the frosted window. We climb up the hillside and into the apples. We don't stop until we see the sign PICKERS WANTED.

All of us kids jump out of the cars and pickups at once. The Hoffman twins are the first to swing from the low branches and we play hide-and-seek in the empty bins. It's easy to find each other because breath clouds tell your hiding place.

Dave is our foreman, and he arrives in a big truck that doesn't have a door. He hands each of us a purple ticket. Then Papa lifts up the lunch chest and we head down to our trees. Grandma and Grandpa are on the same row.

"I'm going to pick a whole bin," I say.

"That's a lot of apples," Papa answers.

"I'm bigger this year."

"No doubt about that," he says.

While Papa sets up the ladders, Mama fastens the canvas bag around my back.

"It's not as heavy as last year," I say.

"There're no apples in it," Mama replies.

"But it's not loose either."

"No, it's not. I don't need to go over as many loops. You've grown."

Even before Papa turns his radio on, I'm up the ladder. Twist! Snap! Twist!
Snap! The apples fall in the bag and rub against my stomach. I remember to lean
into the ladder for balance so both hands are free for picking. That's what
Grandpa taught me.

We work fast in the morning because after lunch we will be hot and tired. Now we wear woolen shirts and gloves with the fingers cut out. Mama says when you go apple picking, you need to keep your hands warm but have a good grip. That's what Grandma taught *her*.

Every few minutes someone yells "Full!" We hear Dave's tractor in the distance. First he stops for Sister Dolores, then Grandpa. Papa is next.

Dave must have known Papa's bin was ready because he drives over while Papa is still up on the ladder. Before he takes the apples away, he punches a half-moon on Papa's ticket.

The tractor comes again and again. Again and again. By lunchtime Mama has two and Papa has three half-moons on their tickets. Mine has none.

I help Papa spread out a worn quilt under a tree, and we make cushions with our heavy shirts. Mama unpacks the food and pours coffee for everyone but me. I have hot chocolate. Grandma always says that food tastes better when you eat outdoors. I think so too. Later, Papa fiddles with the radio buttons, and the music changes.

"Ready?" he asks.

Mama takes Papa's hands, and he brings her to him, almost in a hug, but more graceful. Then he twirls her around under the branches. Mama can spin good even in tennis shoes. Round and round they go. When the music gets soft, Mama loosens her red scarf and brown curls fall down her back. Without stopping, they reach for me, and we are three dancing. The music quickens, and Papa carries me so I won't miss steps. We whirl faster and faster in a circle. As we spin, the trees do too, and I'm sure they must be dizzy from watching us.

The music slows, and Papa sways back and forth,
with one arm around Mama and the other around me. I want
the radio to play forever and our friends to keep clapping.
But the work whistle blows, and Grandpa calls to us.

Even before Papa can turn the music low, I'm up the
ladder. Twist! Snap! Twist! Snap! That bin is almost full.

We pick all afternoon, and still the tractor doesn't come for me. Now the harness straps dig into my shoulders, and the sun is too bright. Papa tries to move the ladder as the sun moves, but the sun always tricks him. Only the little kids napping under the trees have shade.

Near quitting time, our row starts to empty. First, Grandma and Grandpa pack up. Our friends follow soon after. When they go, their radios do too, and except for Dave's tractor in the distance, the orchard is suddenly silent.

In the quiet, a girl's voice calls out "Full!" and her echo answers right back.

"Mama! Papa! It's mine!"

But they are both already beside me.

"Congratulations! Hooray for Anna!"

"Mighty fine job," says Dave as he punches a half-moon on my ticket.

"I guess you'll know what to do with this," he laughs.

I don't take off my canvas bag, and I don't wait for
Mama and Papa. I run all the way to the orchard office to
cash my ticket in. When Grandpa sees me, I get a big hug,
and all the other kids want to see the ticket too.

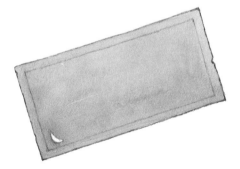

Soon Mama and Papa join us, and everyone loads up their cars and pickups and says good-bye.

Then the procession moves slowly down the hillside away from the apples. We travel past fallen cornstalks, fields of hay, and mailboxes with their flags down. And if we hit a bump, no one mentions it.

Mama and Papa talk in low voices, and I dream about apples,

and dancing, and *two* half-moons on a purple ticket.